Charlie Parker played be bop

Chris Raschka

ORCHARD PAPERBACKS

An Imprint of Scholastic Inc.

This book was originally published in hardcover by Orchard Books in 1992, and in paperback in 1997.

ISBN 0-531-07095-6

12 11 10 9

Printed in the U.S.A.

Book designed by Mina Greenstein.
The text of this book is set in Caslon 540 and Helvetica condensed.
The illustrations are watercolor and charcoal pencil, reproduced in full color.

Library of Congress Cataloging-in-Publication Data
Raschka, Christopher. Charlie Parker played be bop / by Chris Raschka.   p.   cm. Summary: Introduces the famous saxophonist and his style of jazz known as bebop.
ISBN 0-531-05999-5 (tr.)   ISBN 0-531-08599-6 (lib. bdg.)   ISBN 0-531-07095-6 (pbk.)
1. Parker, Charlie, 1920–1955—Juvenile literature. 2. Jazz musicians—United States—Biography—Juvenile literature. [1. Parker, Charlie, 1920–1955. 2. Musicians. 3. Jazz. 4. Afro-Americans—Biography.]
I. Title.   II. Title: Charlie Parker played bebop.   ML3930.P24R4   1992
788.7'3165'092—dc20   [B] 91-38420

To Phil Schaap

Charlie Parker played **be bop.**

Charlie Parker played **saxophone.**

The music sounded like **be bop.**

Never leave your cat alone.

Be bop.

Fisk, fisk.

Lollipop.

Boomba, boomba.

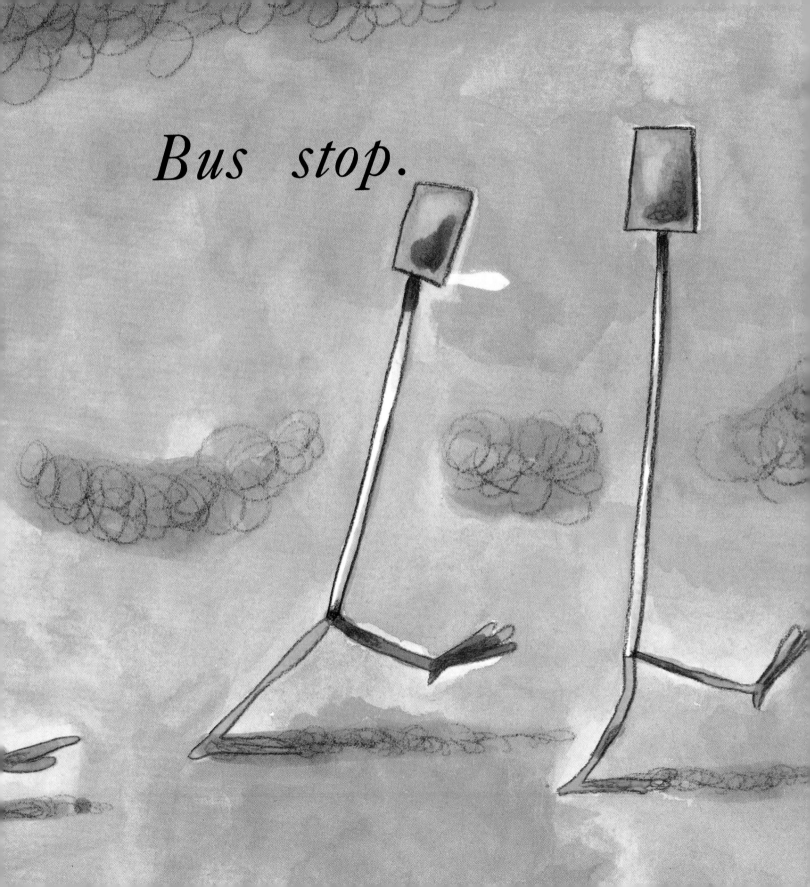

Bus stop.

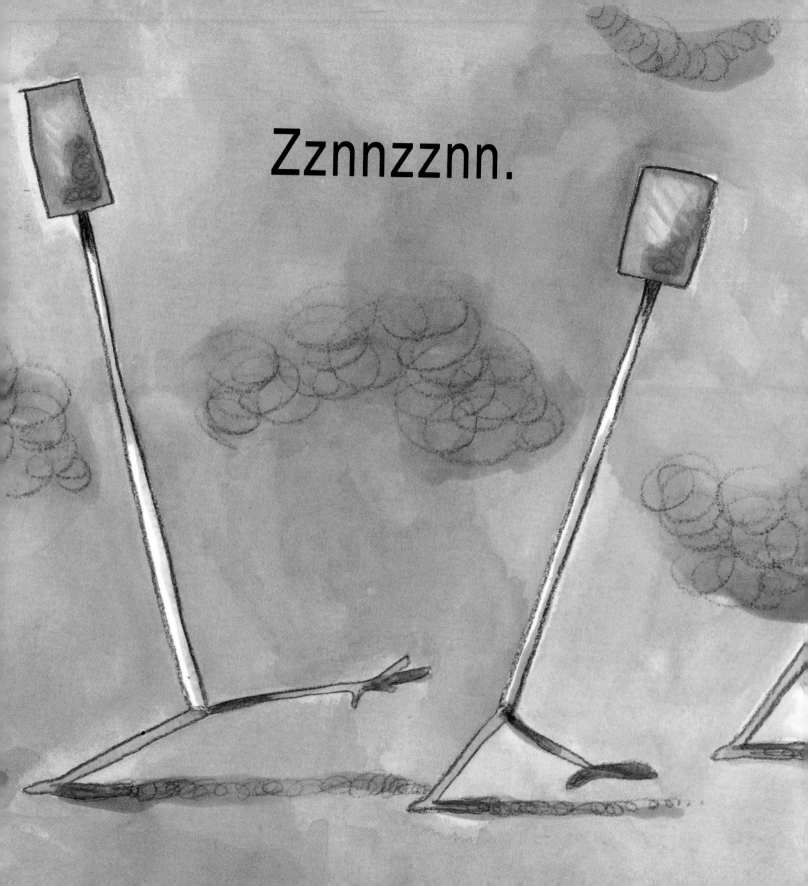

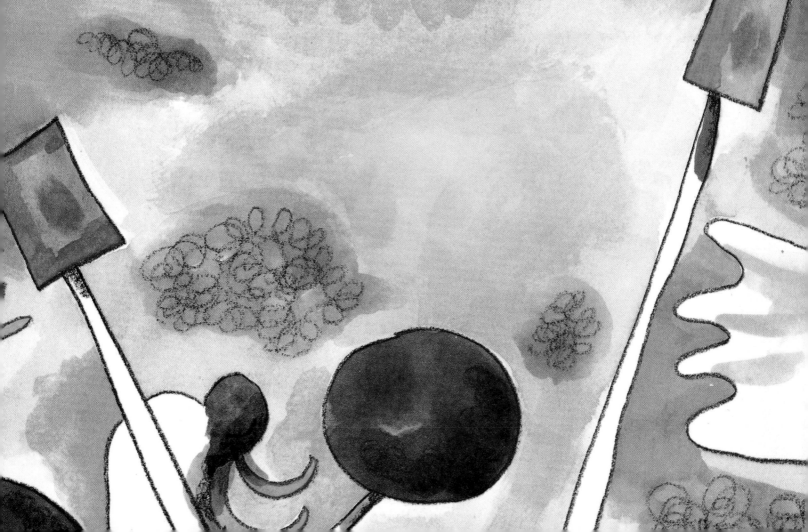

Charlie Parker played **be bop.**

Charlie Parker played no trombone.

The music sounded like be bop.

Barbeque that last leg bone.

Alphabet, alphabet, alphabet, alph,

Chickadee, chickadee, chickadee, chick,

Overshoes, overshoes, overshoes, o,

Reeti-footi, reeti-footi, reeti-footi, ree.

Charlie Parker played be bop.

Charlie Parker played alto saxophone.

The music sounded like hip hop.

Never leave your cat . . .

a-  lone.